SWEET POTATO PIE

BY KATHLEEN D. LINDSEY
ILLUSTRATED BY CHARLOTTE RILEY-WEBB

Lee & Low Books Inc. • New York

In loving memory of our son Darrell Lawrence Lindsey, and for Jaquille, Sade, Natasha, Dean, Donald, and David II, who helped make this book come alive through their wonder years. To all of my precious grandchildren, Jackie, Donny, Douglas, Garrett, David III, and Sarah, who bring me great joy. Thank you David Sr. for 37 years of never letting me give up on my hopes and dreams. —K.D.L.

To the memory of my dear mother, Ruby Nelson-Riley, who always filled our home with the love and aroma of "something sweet." —C.R.-W.

LEE & LOW BOOKS Inc., 95 Madison Avenue, New York, NY 10016
leeandlow.com

Special thanks to author Ferida Wolff and all my dear friends and relatives who encouraged, supported, and reminded me that I can do all things through Christ who strengthens me—Seven Quilts for Seven Sisters, Bill Williams, Wanda Alston, Grace Metz, and author Judy Harch. Many thanks to my literary agent Pema Browne, and executive editor Louise May, for all your hard work and support to help make my dream come true. —K.D.L.

"Sweet Potato Pie" quilt on page 32 by Kathleen D. Lindsey

Manufactured in China by South China Printing Co.

Book design by Tania Garcia
Book production by The Kids at Our House

The text is set in Cheltenham
The illustrations are rendered in acrylic

10 9 8 7 6 5 4 3 2 1
First Edition

Library of Congress Cataloging-in-Publication Data
Lindsey, Kathleen D.
    Sweet potato pie / by Kathleen D. Lindsey ; illustrated by Charlotte Riley-Webb.— 1st ed.
        p. cm.
    Summary: During a drought in the early 1900s, a large loving African American family finds a delicious way to earn the money they need to save their family farm.
    ISBN 1-58430-061-2
    [1. Moneymaking projects—Fiction. 2. Family life—Fiction. 3. Farm life—Fiction. 4. Pies—Fiction. 5. African Americans—Fiction.] I. Riley-Webb, ill. II. Title.
PZ7.L66115 Sw 2003   [E]—dc21   2002030164

I was nearly eight years old when a great drought swept across our county. I had many gardening chores that summer. I hoed the ground, pulled weeds, and picked those wrinkled vegetables that didn't get all the water they needed.

Papa said those were the worst crops he'd ever seen! But finally the cool weather came, bringing the sweet rain, just in time to save our sweet potatoes.

Papa was a hardworking man, but even hard work wasn't enough. Late one morning as we sat in the kitchen, Papa pulled a letter from his pocket. It was a note from the bank, and it said the bank would take away our farm in a month if Papa didn't pay back the money he had borrowed. We owed nearly seventy-five dollars. That was a heap of money!

"We don't even have seventy-five cents. How are we suppose to pay back seventy-five dollars?" Papa said with a worried look on his face.

Papa walked slowly to the backdoor and looked out across the field.

"All we have left are the sweet potatoes," he said. "We'll have to come up with something, or we'll lose our farm."

I looked over at Mama, sitting in her chair sorting scraps of cloth to make a winter quilt. A moment later she put her quilting aside and went to the cupboard. She took out two freshly baked sweet potato pies, seven cracked and chipped cups, and an old teapot with a broken spout.

"Come on, children. Let's have something sweet," Mama said.

Mama always thought something sweet would help us solve our problems.

"Mmm-mm," Papa said, trying not to sound too worried. "I'm a lucky man to have a wife who makes the best sweet potato pies in the county and five hungry children who love to eat them up."

All of a sudden Mama threw her hands in the air.

"Praise the Lord!" she shouted. "I got an idea! Sweet potato pie. Lots of sweet potato pies! Tomorrow and the day after is the Harvest Celebration in town, and people come from miles around. This would be a grand time to sell my sweet potato pies."

"That's a mighty fine idea!" Papa declared, as Mama began to hustle and bustle about the kitchen.

"We all have to work together, now," Mama said. "Everyone will have a job to do."

"I'll take the two older boys with me, and we'll fix up the old wagon to carry the pies," Papa said, and he headed toward the door.

Mama handed Jake and me buckets to fetch milk from our old cow, Lizzy. We ran off to find her while Mama and my big sister, Martha, got busy peeling a mound of sweet potatoes.

"Good morning, Lizzy," Jake said. "I'll be obliged if you was to give us some of your sweet milk for Mama's pies."

Jake was just about done milking Lizzy when she let out a big *moooooo* and started to kick. To calm her down, I commenced to singing and dancing. Then all of a sudden some squealing piglets ran through the barn.

"Watch out, Sadie!" Jake yelled just as I lost my balance and hit one of those buckets with a *BAM!* Milk splashed all over me, head to toe.

After cleaning me up, Mama gave me a large basket and sent me to gather eggs. Who should meet me at the henhouse but our bossy rooster, Rastus. He was strutting around, identifying himself as protector of the coop.

"You better let me in so I can fetch some eggs for Mama's pies," I told Rastus. "Or you might find yourself in Mama's old black cooking pot."

Suddenly Rastus ran toward Jake, who was throwing kernels of corn across the ground to distract him. I slipped into the henhouse and gathered all the eggs I could find. Just as I was coming out, Rastus commenced to chasing me. I ran through the gate as fast as my legs would carry me, trying not to let too many eggs drop to the ground.

Next Jake and me hitched up our half-blind goat, Nanny, and went to fetch a sack of flour at the mill house. On the way back Jake decided to take a shortcut up the rocky hill. Suddenly Nanny tripped and overturned the cart, and that sack of flour came tumbling down the hill aimed straight at me. The sack broke open and covered me with flour.

Mama and Martha were cooking and mashing sweet potatoes when I walked into the kitchen. One look at me and Mama let out a big scream. Then she began to laugh so hard she cried.

"Are you mad at us, Mama?" I asked sadly.

"Now, how can I be upset when I know my babies did their best," Mama said, wiping tears of laughter from her eyes. "I think we have just enough ingredients left to make my sweet potato pies."

Everyone began working together, taking turns churning some of the milk into creamy butter. Next we added sugar, eggs, and milk to the warm potatoes. After adding the spices and beating the filling, Mama poured it into her special, extra-flaky pie crusts. Then into the oven went the pies.

When the last pies were done, we fell into bed, anxious for morning to come.

Cock-a-doodle-do! Cock-a-doodle-do!
We woke up the next morning to the sound of Rastus crowing. After a big breakfast we all dressed in our Sunday best.
    The morning was chilly, so we worked quickly to gather up the heaps of pies wrapped in brown paper and gently carry them outside to the wagon. Mama made sure the pies were packed in just right so there would be room for us children to ride too.

What a sight we saw when we arrived in town! Folks had come from everywhere for the Harvest Celebration.

"This celebration is where hardworking people come together and proudly show off what they grew on their farms or made with their hands," Papa said. "And some win blue ribbons too." He chuckled and looked at Mama out of the corner of his eye.

Everywhere we looked people were selling wonderful things—fruits, vegetables, cakes, pies, jams, toys, quilts, and lots of pretty cloth. But nobody, not anybody, had sweet potato pies but us!

FRESH PRODUCE

We unhitched our wagon and started setting out the pies. Just as we put the last pie in place, the band began to play.

Boom! Boom! Boom! The drums sounded like thunder. *Clang! Clang! Clang!* The big brass cymbals crashed together.

"Pies for sale! Pies for sale! Sweet potato pies for sale!" We all tried shouting over the music, but nobody seemed to notice.

"Pies for sale! My mama's special pies for sale!" I shouted even louder, but everyone kept rushing by us.

"Mama, don't they want our pies?" I asked sorrowfully.

"I don't think they can hear us, Sadie," Mama said. "The band is playing so loud, it's drowning us out."

Suddenly I had an idea. I asked Mama to
unwrap two pies. I took one and handed Jake the other.
   "Follow me," I said, and Jake and me started dancing
through the crowd, carrying the pies above our heads.
   "Pies for sale! Pies for sale! Sweet potato pies for
sale!" we shouted as the sweet smell of the pies began
to fill the air. Soon we were leading a parade of hungry
people back to our wagon, where Mama started giving
out samples for folks to taste.

Ladies commenced to fill their baskets with pies as they chatted with Mama about her recipe. Men said Mama's pie was the best they had ever tasted. Children came running to try a taste too.

Jake collected the money for Mama, and I kept bringing more pies from the wagon. I made sure to tell everyone it was Mama's special, extra-flaky crust that made her pies so good.

After a while Mama and Papa took us to the pie-judging tent, where Papa had secretly entered one of Mama's pies. Everything looked so good.

"Mama! Mama!" we suddenly heard Martha call. "Come quickly."

When we reached Martha, we saw a big blue ribbon on Mama's pie. It had won the prize for best pie at the Harvest Celebration!

"Mercy me!" Mama declared, and we all started whooping and hollering with joy.

Next we went to the General Store to see if Mr. and Mrs. Fields wanted a pie. They bought two and put in an order for ten pies to be delivered every week. The woman at the Sweet Shop ordered a dozen, and the owner of the restaurant told Mama he wanted as many pies as she had time to bake. By nighttime Mama had an order list as long as my arm.

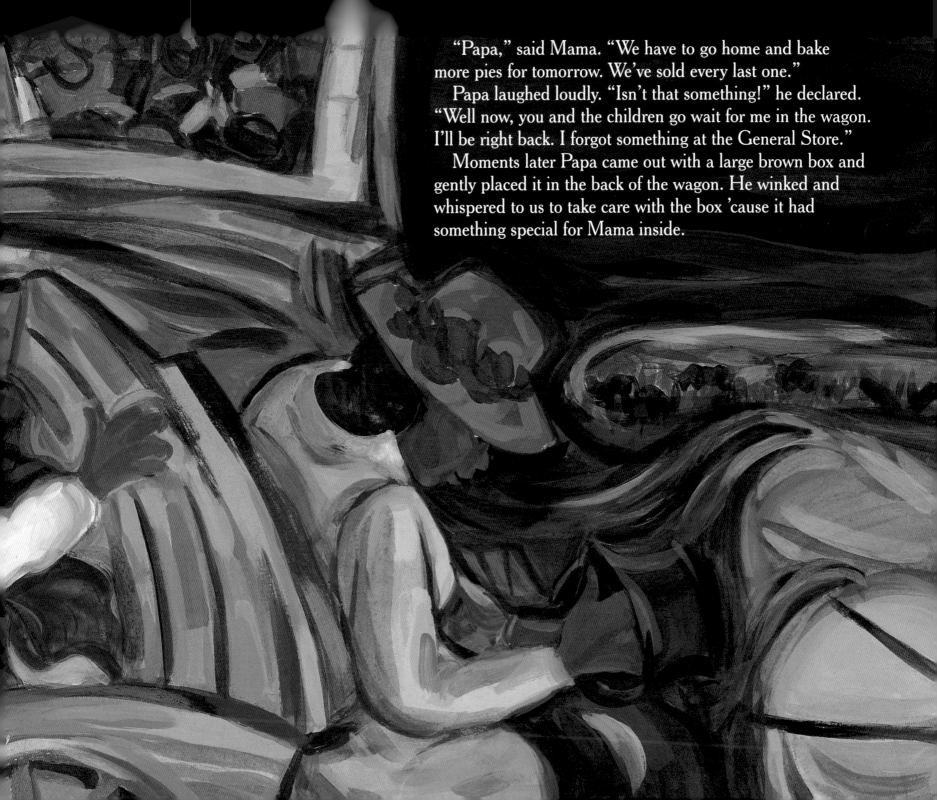

"Papa," said Mama. "We have to go home and bake more pies for tomorrow. We've sold every last one."

Papa laughed loudly. "Isn't that something!" he declared. "Well now, you and the children go wait for me in the wagon. I'll be right back. I forgot something at the General Store."

Moments later Papa came out with a large brown box and gently placed it in the back of the wagon. He winked and whispered to us to take care with the box 'cause it had something special for Mama inside.

We all stayed up late that night helping Mama with the baking. As we sat around the kitchen waiting for the last pies to come out of the oven, Mama set the table with her prettiest tablecloth, Sunday napkins, and the brand-new china tea set Papa had given her as a surprise. Then she commenced to cut thick slices of sweet potato pie.

"Mama, it was mighty clever of you to think of selling pies at the Harvest Celebration," Papa said as we ate our pie and sipped our tea.

Mama smiled. "It's this hardworking family who's clever. With everyone's helping hands, there will always be enough pies to sell."

And that year we made enough money selling Mama's sweet potato pies to save our family farm.

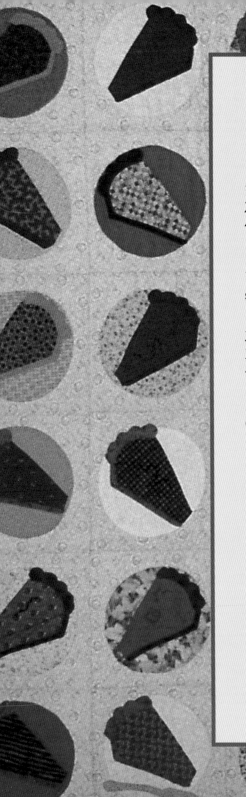
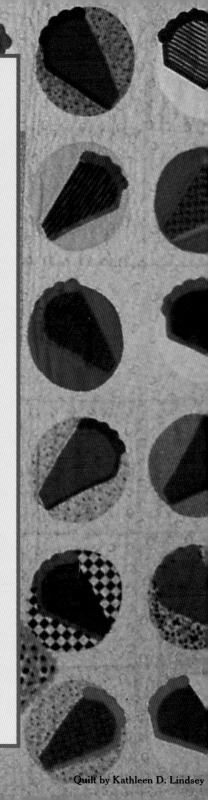

Mama's Sweet Potato Pie*

Children will need adult help

1 Extra-flaky Pie Crust (see recipe below)
1½ pounds sweet potatoes (approximately 3 large)
1 cup sugar
½ cup evaporated milk
2 large eggs
4 tablespoons (½ stick) butter or margarine at room temperature
1 teaspoon ground nutmeg
1 teaspoon vanilla
¼ teaspoon salt
ground cinnamon

1. Preheat oven to 350°F.
2. Peel sweet potatoes and cut into chunks. Boil until tender, about 30 minutes.
3. Drain off water and put hot potatoes into large bowl. Mash potatoes.
4. Add all remaining ingredients except cinnamon and beat sweet potato
   mixture until smooth.
5. Pour warm filling into pie crust and sprinkle top with cinnamon.
6. Bake for about 1 hour, until filling is firm and crust is golden brown.
7. Let cool on rack.

Mama's Extra-Flaky Pie Crust*

1 cup all-purpose flour
½ teaspoon salt
6 tablespoons solid vegetable shortening
¼ cup cold milk

1. Combine flour and salt in bowl.
2. Add shortening and use pastry blender or fork to cut shortening into flour
   mixture until crumbly.
3. Add milk and knead dough until soft ball forms.
4. Roll out dough on lightly floured surface to form large circle.
5. Place circle of dough into 9-inch pie pan and press dough into corners.
6. Trim off excess dough with knife. Use fork to press down around rim of
   pan to create decorative edge.

Quilt by Kathleen D. Lindsey